ROAD TRIP

adapted by
ADAM
BEECHEN

illustrated by
HEATHER
MARTINEZ

based on the movie written by
DEREK DRYMON, TIM HILL,
STEVE HILLENBURG,
KENT OSBORNE,
AARON SPRINGER,
and PAUL TIBBITT

2-GO

SCHOLASTIC INC.
New York Toronto London Auckland Sydney
Mexico City New Delhi Hong Kong Buenos Aires

Based on *The SpongeBob SquarePants Movie* by Nickelodeon Movies and Paramount Pictures

ISBN 0-439-66692-9

12 11 10 9 8 7 6 5 4 3 2 1   4 5 6 7 8 9/0

Printed in the U.S.A.   40

First Scholastic printing, November 2004

Hi there! I'm SpongeBob SquarePants. My best friend, Patrick Star, and I just got back from the wildest, wackiest, weirdest trip any travelers ever traveled!

Would you like to hear about the trip?

I know you do as sure as I know my name is SpongeBob SquarePants. So turn the page, put on the special glasses, and get ready for the ride of your life! Yippee!

It all started when Plankton played a trick on my boss, Mr. Krabs. Plankton stole King Neptune's crown and hid it in faraway Shell City. Then he blamed it on Mr. Krabs!

King Neptune was really mad. He said he was going to cook Mr. Krabs. But then Patrick and I told him we'd go to Shell City to get the crown back.

Patrick and I decided to drive Mr. Krabs's Patty Wagon to Shell City. He wasn't using it. . . . King Neptune had frozen Mr. Krabs in a block of ice! We had to clean out the Patty Wagon before we could drive away. There was a lot of stuff inside, and we just couldn't eat all of it!

We had just stopped to
fill the Patty Wagon with gas,
when it was stolen!

Without the Patty Wagon,
we thought we would have to
walk all the way to Shell City!

Luckily we found the thief and the Patty Wagon! We distracted him with soap bubbles and the Goofy Goobers theme song so we could get the keys to the Patty Wagon back.

"I'm a goofy goober, yeah! You're a goofy goober, yeah! We're all goofy goobers, yeah! Goofy, goofy, goober, goober, yeah!" we sang.

All that singing made us hungry, so Patrick and I stopped at an ice-cream hut and asked the lady behind the counter for banana splits with sprinkles, fairy stars, goober beans, and extra sauce.

It turns out she wasn't a nice lady at all. She was a giant frogfish with a giant appetite!

"You enjoy eating that banana split," she said to me. "I'm going to enjoy eating *you*!"

"Aaaaaaggggghhhhh!!!" I said.

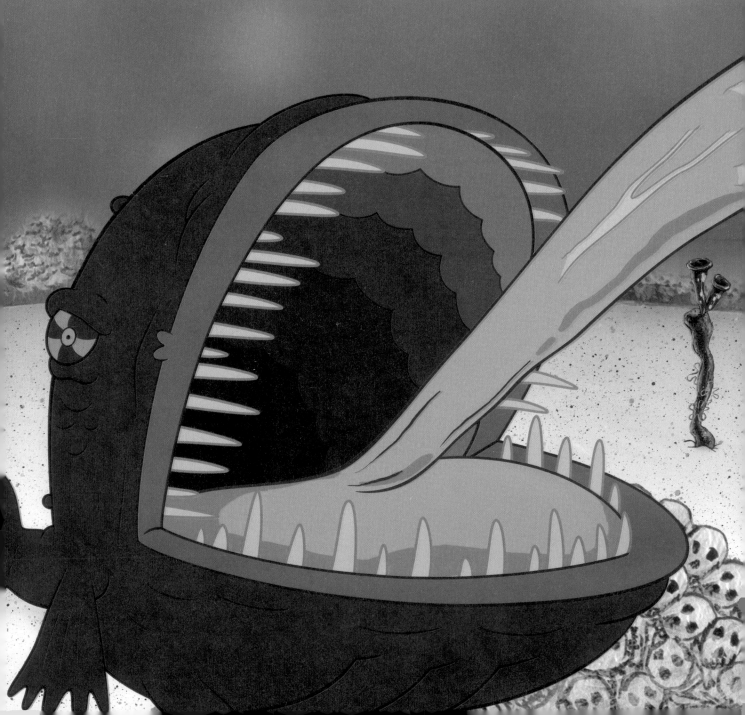

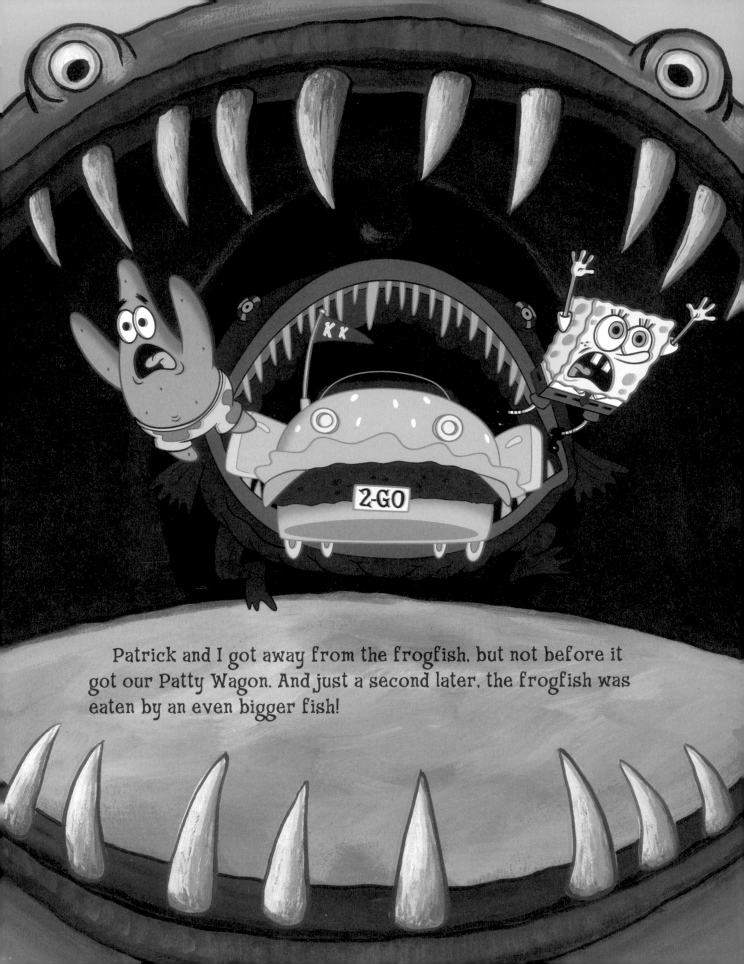

Patrick and I got away from the frogfish, but not before it got our Patty Wagon. And just a second later, the frogfish was eaten by an even bigger fish!

Next we came to a really big trench. The only way to get to Shell City was for us to cross the trench. Patrick and I were scared. We were about to give up and go home when King Neptune's daughter, Mindy, caught up to us!

"We're just kids, Mindy!" I told her. "Going to Shell City is a man's job."

"But Plankton is controlling the minds of everyone in Bikini Bottom with Chum Bucket helmets! You have to save the crown, and the citizens of Bikini Bottom!" she said.

Mindy told us to be brave. She used her mermaid magic to give us manly moustaches and gave us courage to cross the trench!

Patrick and I felt invincible on our journey
now! Monster fish couldn't stop us!

Mountains of rock and stone couldn't stop us!

A stampede of wild sea horses couldn't stop us!

We were on our way to Shell City to get the crown and save Mr. Krabs. *Nothing* was going to stop us!

But this guy Dennis stopped us. He was big and tough, and he wanted to keep Patrick and me from getting to Shell City!

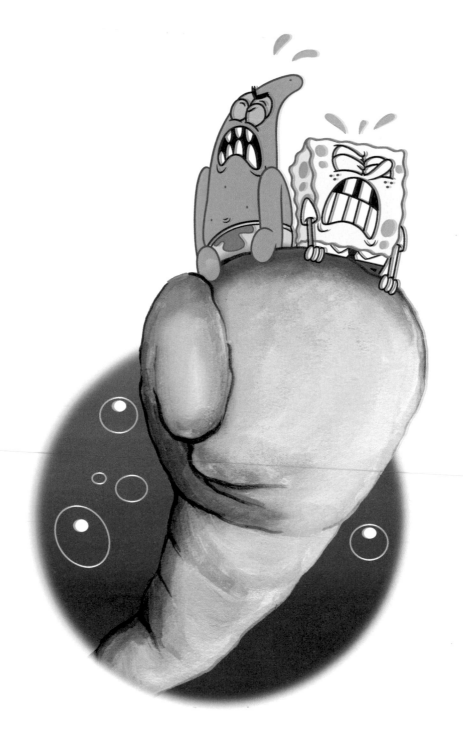

Suddenly a giant cyclops pushed Dennis out of the way!
We were saved! Hooray!
   But then the cyclops grabbed us! We were doomed! Argh!

The cyclops took Patrick and me to Shell City.
The cyclops was going to turn us into googly-eyed gifts! We saw King Neptune's crown on the wall behind him, but we were too dried out to move.

I was upset. Luckily, my tears caused a spark that set off the sprinkler system in Shell City. Water rained down on us, giving us the strength to grab King Neptune's crown and run away!

Patrick and I didn't know how we were going to get back to Bikini Bottom to save Mr. Krabs. Suddenly a lifeguard appeared and told us he'd give us a ride. Hooray!

I wasn't excited for very long, though. That's because Dennis came back, and he really didn't want us to get back to Bikini Bottom with the crown!

I'm not a fighter! I'm a sponge! But I did my best to keep Dennis from getting us. I even offered him my bubbles!

Dennis was just about to finish us—when a boat suddenly came out of nowhere! I never saw the sailor, but if I ever meet him, I'm going to give him a big, spongy hug!

The boat bonked Dennis in the head, and that was the last we saw of him!

Once we got to a spot over Bikini Bottom, the lifeguard gave us an extra push and sent us speeding back home.

We made it back in time to keep King Neptune from cooking Mr. Krabs....

But all of our friends were under Plankton's control, thanks to his Chum Bucket helmets! We were captured faster than you can say, "Goofy Goober!" Plankton told us there was no way we could beat him, since we were only kids!

But Patrick and I were kids who had gone all the way to Shell City!
We had beaten the Cyclops! We had brought back the crown!
So I sang, "I'm a goofy goober, yeah! You're a goofy goober, yeah!
We're all goofy goobers, yeah! Goofy, goofy, goober, goober, yeah!"

The song worked! Plankton was taken to jail, Mr. Krabs was freed, and Patrick and I got to put the crown back on King Neptune's head! We were heroes! Not bad for a couple of kids, huh?